P9-BZF-503

Cici #1
A Fairy's Tale

BELIEVE YOUR EYES

Written by
Cori Doerrfeld

Illustrated by
**Tyler Page and
Cori Doerrfeld**

GRAPHIC UNIVERSE™ • MINNEAPOLIS

Graphic Universe™
A division of Lerner Publishing Group, Inc.
241 First Avenue North
Minneapolis, MN 55401 USA

For reading levels and more information, look up this title at www.lernerbooks.com.

Main body text set in CCDaveGibbonsLower 10/11.
Typeface provided by ComicCraft.

Library of Congress Cataloging-in-Publication Data

The Cataloging-in-Publication Data for Believe Your Eyes is on file at the Library of Congress.
ISBN 978-1-4677-6152-9 (lib. bdg.)
ISBN 978-1-4677-9571-5 (pbk.)
ISBN 978-1-4677-9572-2 (EB pdf)

Manufactured in the United States of America
1 - CG - 12/31/15

For Charlotte

—C.D. & T.P.

6

7

...I can pretty much do it all.

So this is real? You...me... we're...

Fairies.

Cici?!

Coming!

What about Mom? Does that mean she's a fairy too?

No. Your mother chose a different path. But that's another story for another day.

Aren't you going to explain any of this?!

Explain what?

Didn't you notice Mom? Or Sofia?

I choose to believe.

About the Author and Illustrator

Cori Doerrfeld is a freelance author and illustrator who holds degrees from St. Olaf College and the Minneapolis College of Art and Design. She has written and illustrated several picture books, including *Penny Loves Pink, Little Bunny Foo Foo: The Real Story, Matilda in the Middle*, and *Maggie and Wendel*. She lives in Minneapolis with her comic artist husband, Tyler Page, and their two children, Charlotte and Leo. You can follow Cori's work on her website: www.coridoerrfeld.com.

Tyler Page is an Eisner-nominated and Xeric Grant-winning artist and educator. In addition to publishing his own work, he illustrated the *Graphic Universe* series Chicagoland Detective Agency and has created comics and illustrations for a variety of commercial clients. He is also the director of Print Technology Services at the Minneapolis College of Art and Design. He lives in Minneapolis with his wife, author/illustrator Cori Doerrfeld, and their two children.